For Gary Condes and Dan Turner

Scholastic Children's Books
Commonwealth House, 1-19 New Oxford Street
London WC1A 1NU, UK
a division of Scholastic Ltd
London ~ New York ~ Toronto ~ Sydney ~ Auckland
Mexico City ~ New Delhi ~ Hong Kong

First published in hardback in the UK by Scholastic Ltd, 2004

ISBN 0 439 97750 9

Printed in Singapore

2 4 6 8 10 9 7 5 3 1

Cat Trap!

Greg Gormley

SCHOLASTIC
PRESS

"Wake up, Cat!
We'll be late to meet your cousin
at the train station."

“Don’t worry,” said Cat.

"Look out, Cat!
There's a big bad dog
behind you and he doesn't
look very friendly."

“Don’t worry,” said Cat.

"Shhh, be careful, Cat!
There are **TWO** dogs now,
and they look like trouble to me."

"Don't worry," said Cat.

"Don't look now, Cat,
but there are **THREE**
dogs on your tail!"

“Don’t worry,” said Cat.

"I know you think I'm being silly, Cat . . .

. . . but if you don't start listening soon, then you'll be sorry."

“Don’t worry,” said Cat.

"Hold on, where are they?
Phew! I think they've gone!"

"Eeek! **FOUR** dogs! **HELP!**"

“Don’t worry,” said Cat.

"But look!
One, two, three, four . . . **FIVE!**

YOU'RE TRAPPED, CAT!"

"Don't worry," said Cat.

“Here comes my cousin,
and he’s . . .

. . . a TIGER!"

Grrrr!
Grrrr!

Gulp!

Yikes!

"Hello, Tiger," said Cat.
"Hello, Cat," said Tiger.

"BYE BYE, DOGS!"